In 1935 if you wanted to read a good book, you needed either a lot of money or a library card. Cheap paperbacks were available, but their poor production generally mirrored the quality between the covers. One weekend that year, Allen Lane, Managing Director of The Bodley Head, having spent the weekend visiting Agatha Christie, found himself on a platform at Exeter station trying to find something to read for his journey back to London. He was appalled by the quality of the material he had to choose from. Everything that Allen Lane achieved from that day until his death in 1970 was based on a passionate belief in the existence of 'a vast reading public for *intelligent* books at a low price'. The result of his momentous vision was the birth not only of Penguin, but of the 'paperback revolution'. Quality writing became available for the price of a packet of cigarettes, literature became a mass medium for the first time, a nation of book-borrowers became a nation of book-buyers – and the very concept of book publishing was changed for ever. Those founding principles – of quality and value, with an overarching belief in the fundamental importance of reading – have guided everything the company has done since 1935. Sir Allen Lane's pioneering spirit is still very much alive at Penguin in 2005. Here's to the next 70 years!

MORE THAN A BUSINESS

'We decided it was time to end the almost customary half-hearted manner in which cheap editions were produced – as though the only people who could possibly want cheap editions must belong to a lower order of intelligence. We, however, believed in the existence in this country of a vast reading public for intelligent books at a low price, and staked everything on it'
Sir Allen Lane, 1902–1970

'The Penguin Books are splendid value for sixpence, so splendid that if other publishers had any sense they would combine against them and suppress them'
George Orwell

'More than a business ... a national cultural asset'
Guardian

'When you look at the whole Penguin achievement you know that it constitutes, in action, one of the more democratic successes of our recent social history'
Richard Hoggart

Seventeen Poisoned Englishmen

GABRIEL GARCÍA MÁRQUEZ

PENGUIN BOOKS

PENGUIN BOOKS

Published by the Penguin Group
Penguin Books Ltd, 80 Strand, London WC2R 0RL, England
Penguin Group (USA) Inc., 375 Hudson Street, New York, New York 10014, USA
Penguin Group (Canada), 10 Alcorn Avenue, Toronto, Ontario, Canada M4V 3B2
(a division of Pearson Penguin Canada Inc.)
Penguin Ireland, 25 St Stephen's Green, Dublin 2, Ireland
(a division of Penguin Books Ltd)
Penguin Group (Australia), 250 Camberwell Road, Camberwell, Victoria 3124,
Australia (a division of Pearson Australia Group Pty Ltd)
Penguin Books India Pvt Ltd, 11 Community Centre,
Panchsheel Park, New Delhi – 110 017, India
Penguin Group (NZ), cnr Airborne and Rosedale Roads, Albany,
Auckland 1310, New Zealand (a division of Pearson New Zealand Ltd)
Penguin Books (South Africa) (Pty) Ltd, 24 Sturdee Avenue,
Rosebank 2196, South Africa

Penguin Books Ltd, Registered Offices: 80 Strand, London WC2R 0RL, England

www.penguin.com

Collected Stories first published in Great Britain by Jonathan Cape 1991
Strange Pilgrims first published in Great Britain by Jonathan Cape 1993
This selection published as a Pocket Penguin 2005
2

Set in 11/13pt Monotype Dante
Typeset by Palimpsest Book Production Limited,
Polmont, Stirlingshire
Printed in England by Clays Ltd, St Ives plc

Contents

Seventeen Poisoned Englishmen

The first thing Señora Prudencia Linero noticed when she reached the port of Naples was that it had the same smell as the port of Riohacha. She did not tell anyone, of course, since no one would have understood on that senile ocean liner filled to overflowing with Italians from Buenos Aires who were returning to their native land for the first time since the war, but in any case, at the age of seventy-two, and at a distance of eighteen days of heavy seas from her people and her home, she felt less alone, less frightened and remote.

The lights on land had been visible since daybreak. The passengers got up earlier than usual, wearing new clothes, their hearts heavy with the uncertainties of putting ashore, so that the last Sunday on board seemed to be the only genuine one of the entire voyage. Señora Prudencia Linero was one of the very few who attended Mass. In contrast to the clothes she had worn before, when she walked around the ship dressed in partial mourning, today she had on a tunic of coarse brown burlap tied with the cord of Saint Francis, and rough leather sandals that did not resemble a pilgrim's only because they were too new. It was an advance payment: She had promised God that she would wear the full-length habit for the rest of her life if He blessed her with a trip to Rome to see the Supreme Pontiff, and she already considered the blessing granted. When Mass was over she lit a candle to the Holy Spirit in gratitude for the infusion of courage that had allowed her to endure the Caribbean storms, and she said a prayer for each of her nine children and fourteen grandchildren who at that very moment were dreaming about her on a windy night in Riohacha.

When she went up on deck after breakfast, life on the ship had changed. Luggage was piled in the ballroom, along with all kinds of tourist trinkets the Italians had bought at the magic markets of the Antilles, and on the saloon bar there was a macaque from Pernambuco in a wrought-iron cage. It was a brilliant morning in early August. One of those exemplary postwar summer Sundays when the light was like a daily revelation, and the enormous ship inched along, with an invalid's labored breathing, through a transparent stillwater. The gloomy fortress of the Dukes of Anjou was just beginning to loom on the horizon, but the passengers who had come on deck thought they recognized familiar places, and they pointed at them without quite seeing them, shouting with joy in their southern dialects. To her surprise, Señora Prudencia Linero, who had made so many dear old friends on board, who had watched children while their parents danced, and even sewn a button on the first officer's tunic, found them all distant and changed. The social spirit and human warmth that permitted her to survive her first homesickness in the stifling heat of the tropics had disappeared. The eternal loves of the high seas ended when the port came into view. Señora Prudencia Linero, who was not familiar with the voluble nature of Italians, thought the problem lay not in the hearts of others but in her own, since she was the only one going in a crowd that was returning. Every voyage must be like this, she thought, suffering for the first time in her life the sharp pain of being a foreigner, while she leaned on the railing and contemplated the vestiges of so many extinct worlds in the depths of the water. All at once a very beautiful girl standing beside her startled her with a scream of horror.

'*Mamma mia*,' she cried, pointing down. 'Look over there.'

It was a drowned man. Señora Prudencia Linero saw him drifting faceup, a mature, bald man of rare natural distinction, with open, joyful eyes the color of the sky at dawn. He wore full evening dress with a brocade vest, patent-leather shoes, and a fresh gardenia in his lapel. In his right hand he held a little square package wrapped in gift paper, and his pale iron fingers clutched at the bow, which was all he had found to hold on to at the moment of his death.

'He must have fallen from a wedding party,' said one of the ship's officers. 'It happens pretty often in these waters during the summer.'

It was a momentary vision, because just then they were entering the bay, and other, less mournful subjects distracted the attention of the passengers. But Señora Prudencia Linero continued to think about the drowned man, the poor drowned man, whose long-tailed jacket rippled in their wake.

As soon as the ship sailed into the harbor, a decrepit tugboat came out to meet it and lead it by the nose through the wreckage of countless military craft destroyed during the war. The water was turning into oil as the ship made its way past the rusting wrecks, and the heat became even fiercer than in Riohacha at two in the afternoon. On the other side of the narrow channel, the city, brilliant in the eleven-o'clock sun, came into view with all its chimerical palaces and ancient, painted hovels crowded together on the hills. Just then an unbearable stench rose from the disturbed bottom, which Señora Prudencia Linero recognized from the courtyard of her house as the foul breath of rotting crabs.

While this maneuver took place, the passengers, with great displays of joy, recognized their relatives in the tumultuous crowd on the pier. Most of them were autumnal matrons with dazzling bosoms who suffocated in their mourning clothes and had the most beautiful and numerous children in the world, and small, diligent husbands, the immortal kind who read the newspaper after their wives and dress like stern notaries despite the heat.

In the midst of that carnival confusion, a very old man wearing a beggar's overcoat and an inconsolable expression pulled a profusion of tiny chicks from his pockets with both hands. In an instant they covered the entire pier, crazed and cheeping, and it was only because they were magic that many survived and kept running after being stepped on by the crowd that was oblivious to the miracle. The wizard had placed his hat upside down on the ground, but nobody at the railing tossed him even one charitable coin.

Fascinated by the wondrous spectacle that seemed to be presented in her honor, for only she appreciated it, Señora Prudencia Linero was not aware of the exact moment when the gangplank was lowered and a human avalanche invaded the ship with the howling momentum of a pirate attack. Dazed by the wild jubilation and the rancid-onion smell of so many families in summer, shoved by the gangs of porters who came to blows over the baggage, she felt threatened by the same inglorious death that menaced the little chicks on the pier. That was when she sat down on her wooden trunk with its painted tin corners and remained there undaunted, intoning a vicious circle of prayers against temptation and danger in the lands of infidels. The first officer found her when the cataclysm had passed and she was the only one left in the abandoned ballroom.

'Nobody's supposed to be here now,' the officer told her with a certain amiability. 'Can I help you with something?'

'I have to wait for the consul,' she said.

That was true. Two days before she sailed, her oldest son had sent a telegram to his friend the consul in Naples, asking him to meet his mother at the port and help her through the procedures for continuing on to Rome. He had told him the name of the ship and the time of its arrival, and that he would recognize her because she would be wearing the habit of Saint Francis when she came ashore. She was so uncompromising about these arrangements that the first officer allowed her to wait a little longer, although soon it would be time for the crew's lunch, and they had already put the chairs on the tables and were washing down the decks with buckets of water. They had to move her trunk several times in order not to wet it, but she changed places without changing expression, without interrupting her prayers, until they took her out of the recreation rooms and left her sitting in the full sun among the lifeboats. That was where the first officer found her again a little before two, drowning in sweat inside her penitent's garb, saying the Rosary with no expectations because she was terrified and sad and it was all she could do not to cry.

'It's useless for you to keep praying,' said the officer, without his former amiability. 'Even God goes on vacation in August.'

He explained that at this time of year half of Italy was at the beach, above all on Sundays. In all likelihood the consul was not on vacation, given the nature of his responsibilities, but it was certain he would not open the office until Monday. The only reasonable thing was to go to a hotel, get a good night's sleep, and telephone the consulate the next day; no doubt the number was in the phone book. Señora Prudencia Linero had no choice but to accept his judgment, and the officer helped her through the procedures for immigration and customs and changing money, and put her in a taxi, with vague instructions that she be taken to a decent hotel.

The decrepit taxi, with its traces of a funeral carriage, lurched down the deserted streets. For a moment Señora Prudencia Linero thought she and the driver were the only living creatures in a city of ghosts that hung from clotheslines in the middle of the street, but she also thought that a man who talked so much, and with so much passion, could not have time to harm a poor solitary woman who had risked the dangers of the ocean to see the Pope.

At the end of the labyrinth of streets she saw the sea again. The taxi continued to lurch along a burning, deserted beach where there were numerous small hotels painted in bright colors. It did not stop at any of these but drove straight to the least gaudy one, which was situated in a public garden with large palm trees and green benches. The driver placed the trunk on the shaded side-walk, and when he saw Señora Prudencia Linero's uncertainty, he assured her that this was the most decent hotel in Naples.

A handsome, kindhearted porter hoisted the trunk on his shoulder and took charge of her. He led her to the metal grillwork elevator that had been improvised in the stairwell, and with alarming determination began to sing a Puccini aria at the top of his voice. It was a venerable building, with a different hotel on each of its nine renovated floors. All at once, in a kind of hallucination, Señora Prudencia Linero felt that she was in a chicken cage rising slowly through the center of an echoing marble staircase, catching glimpses of people in their houses with their most intimate misgivings, with their torn underwear and acidic belches. On the third floor the elevator jolted to a halt, and then the porter stopped singing, opened the sliding rhomboids of the door, and with a gallant bow indicated to Señora Prudencia Linero that she was in her house.

In the foyer she saw a languid adolescent behind a wooden counter with insets of colored glass and shade plants in copper pots. She liked him at once because he had the same angelic ringlets as her youngest grandson. She liked the name of the hotel, with its letters engraved on a bronze plaque, she liked the odor of carbolic acid, she liked the hanging ferns, the silence, the golden fleurs-de-lis on the wallpaper. Then she stepped out of the elevator, and her heart sank. A group of English tourists wearing shorts and beach sandals were dozing in a long row of easy chairs. There were seventeen of them, seated in symmetrical order, as if they were only one man repeated many times in a hall of mirrors. Señora Prudencia Linero took them in at a single glance without distinguishing one from the other, and all she could see was the long row of pink knees that looked like slabs of pork hanging from hooks in a butcher shop. She did not take another step toward the counter, but retreated in consternation into the elevator.

'Let's go to another floor,' she said.

'This is the only one that has a dining room, Signora,' said the porter.

'It doesn't matter,' she said.

The porter made a gesture of consent, closed the elevator, and sang the remaining portion of the song until they came to the hotel on the fifth floor. Everything seemed less rigorous here, the owner was a springlike matron who spoke fluent Spanish, and no one was taking a siesta in the easy chairs in the foyer. There was in fact no dining room, but the hotel had arranged with a nearby restaurant to serve the guests at a reduced price. And so Señora Prudencia Linero decided yes, she would stay for one night, persuaded as much by the owner's eloquence and amiability as by her relief that not a single Englishman with pink knees was sleeping in the foyer.

At three in the afternoon the blinds in her room were closed, and the half-shadow preserved the cool silence of a hidden grove, and it was a good place to cry. As soon as she was alone, Señora Prudencia Linero bolted both locks, and for the first time since the morning she urinated, in a thin, hesitant stream that allowed her to recover the identity she had lost during the journey. Then she removed her sandals and the cord around her waist, and lay down on her left side on the double bed that was too wide and too lonely for her alone, and released the other flood of long-overdue tears.

Not only was this the first time she had left Riohacha, but it was one of the few times she had left her house after her children married and moved away, and she was alone with two barefoot Indian women to care for the soulless body of her husband. Half her life had been spent in the bedroom facing the ruins of the only man she ever loved, who for almost thirty years had been in a coma, lying on a goatskin mattress in the bed of their youthful lovemaking.

During the previous October, the invalid had opened his eyes in a sudden flash of lucidity, recognized his family, and asked them to send for a photographer. They brought in the old man from the park with the enormous bellows and black-sleeve camera and the magnesium plate for taking pictures in the home. The sick man himself arranged the photographs. 'One for Prudencia, for the love and happiness she gave me in life,' he said. This was taken with the first magnesium flash. 'Now another two for my darling daughters, Prudencita and Natalia,' he said. These were taken. 'Another two for my sons, whose affection and good judgment make them examples to the family,' he said. And so on until the photographer ran out of paper and had to go home for a new supply. At four o'clock, when the magnesium smoke and the tumultuous crowd of relatives, friends, and acquaintances who flocked to receive their copies of the portrait made the air in the bedroom unbreathable, the invalid began to lose consciousness in his bed, and he waved good-bye to everyone as if he were erasing himself from the world at the railing of a ship.

His death was not the relief for the widow that everyone had hoped for. On the contrary, she was so grief-stricken that her children gathered to ask what they could do to comfort her, and she replied that all she wanted was to go to Rome to meet the Pope.

'I'll go alone and wear the habit of Saint Francis,' she informed them. 'I've made a vow.'

The only gratification remaining from those years of vigil was the pleasure of crying. On the ship, when she had to share her cabin with two Clarissine sisters who went ashore at Marseilles, she would linger in the bathroom to cry unseen. As a result the hotel room in Naples was the only suitable place she had found since leaving Riohacha where she could cry to her heart's content. And she would have cried until the following day, when the train left for Rome, if the owner had not knocked at her door at seven to say that if she did not go to the restaurant soon she would have nothing to eat.

The porter accompanied her. A cool breeze had begun to blow in from the sea, and there were still some bathers on the beach under the pale seven-o'clock sun. Señora Prudencia Linero followed the porter along a difficult terrain of steep, narrow streets that were just beginning to wake from their Sunday siesta, and then found herself in a shaded arbor where the tables were covered with red-checkered cloths and jars served as vases for paper flowers. At that early hour her only fellow diners were the waiters and waitresses and a very poor priest eating bread and onions at a back table. When she went in she felt everyone's eyes on her brown habit, but this did not affect her, for she knew that ridicule was part of her penance. The waitress, on the other hand, roused a spark of pity in her, because she was blonde and beautiful and spoke as if she were singing, and Señora Prudencia Linero thought that things must be very bad in Italy after the war if a girl like her had to wait on tables in a restaurant. But she felt at ease in the flowering arbor, and the aroma of stew with bay leaf from the kitchen awakened the hunger that had been deferred by the anxieties of the day. For the first time in a long while she had no desire to cry.

And yet she could not eat as she wished, in part because it was difficult to communicate with the blonde waitress, even though she was kind and patient, and in part because some little songbirds, the kind kept in cages in the houses of Riohacha, were the only meat available. The priest who was eating in the corner, and later acted as interpreter, tried to make her understand that the emergencies of war had not ended in Europe, and the fact that at least there were little woodland birds to eat ought to be viewed as a miracle. But she pushed them away.

'For me,' she said, 'it would be like eating one of my children.'

And so she had to settle for some vermicelli soup, a plate of squash boiled with a few shreds of rancid bacon, and a piece of bread as hard as marble. While she was eating, the priest approached her table to ask in the name of charity that she buy him a cup of coffee, and he sat down with her. He was from Yugoslavia but had been a missionary in Bolivia, and spoke an awkward, expressive Spanish. To Señora Prudencia Linero he seemed an ordinary man with no vestige of God's indulgence, and she observed that he had disgraceful hands with broken, dirty nails, and an onion breath so persistent it seemed more like a character trait. But he was in the service of God, after all, and it was a pleasure as well, when she was so far from home, to meet someone she could talk to.

They conversed at their leisure, oblivious to the heavy barnyard noise that began to surround them as more people sat at the other tables. Señora Prudencia Linero already had a definitive opinion of Italy: She did not like it. And not because the men were somewhat improper, which was saying a great deal, or because they ate songbirds, which was going too far, but because they were in the wicked habit of leaving drowned men to drift in the water.

The priest, who had ordered a *grappa* at her expense along with the coffee, tried to make her see the superficiality of her opinion. For during the war they had established a very efficient service for rescuing, identifying, and burying in holy ground the many drowning victims found floating in the Bay of Naples.

'Centuries ago,' the priest concluded, 'the Italians learned that there is only one life, and they try to live it the best they can. This has made them calculating and talkative, but it has also cured them of cruelty.'

'They didn't even stop the ship,' she said.

'What they do is radio the port authorities,' said the priest. 'By now they've picked him up and buried him in the name of God.'

The discussion changed both their moods. Señora Prudencia Linero had finished eating, and only then did she realize that all the tables were occupied. At the ones close by, almost naked tourists sat eating in silence, among them a few couples who kissed and did not eat. At the tables in the rear, near the bar, neighborhood people played at dice and drank a colorless wine. Señora Prudencia Linero understood that she had only one reason for being in that unsavory country.

'Do you think it will be very difficult to see the Pope?' she asked.

The priest replied that nothing was easier in the summer. The Pope was on vacation in Castel Gandolfo, and on Wednesday afternoons he held a public audience for pilgrims from all over the world. The entrance fee was very cheap: twenty lire.

'And how much does he charge to hear a person's confession?' she asked.

'The Holy Father does not hear confessions,' said the priest, somewhat scandalized, 'except for those of kings, of course.'

'I don't see why he would refuse that favor to a poor woman who's come so far,' she said.

'And some kings, even though they're kings, have died waiting,' said the priest. 'But tell me: Yours must be an awful sin if you made such a journey all alone just to confess to the Holy Father.'

Señora Prudencia Linero thought for a moment, and the priest saw her smile for the first time.

'Mother of God!' she said. 'I'd be satisfied just to see him.' And she added, with a sigh that seemed to come from her soul: 'It's been my lifelong dream!'

The truth was that she still felt frightened and sad, and all she wanted was to leave the restaurant, as well as Italy, without delay. The priest must have thought he had gotten all he could from the deluded woman, and so he wished her good luck and went to another table to ask in the name of charity that they buy him a cup of coffee.

When she walked out of the restaurant, Señora Prudencia Linero found a changed city. She was surprised by the sunlight at nine o'clock, and frightened by the raucous throng that had invaded the streets to find relief in the evening breeze. The backfiring of so many crazed Vespas made life impossible. Driven by bare-chested men whose beautiful women sat behind them, hugging them around the waist, they moved in fits and starts, weaving in and out among hanging pigs and tables covered with melons.

It was a carnival atmosphere, but it seemed a catastrophe to Señora Prudencia Linero. She lost her way, and all at once found herself in an infelicitous street where taciturn women sat in the doorways of identical houses whose blinking red lights made her shiver with terror. A well-dressed man wearing a heavy gold ring and a diamond in his tie followed her for several blocks saying something in Italian, and then in English and French. When he received no reply, he showed her a postcard from a pack he took out of his pocket, and one glance was all she needed to feel that she was walking through hell.

She fled in utter terror, and at the end of the street she found the twilight sea again and the same stink of rotting shellfish as in the port of Riohacha, and her heart returned to its rightful place. She recognized the painted hotels along the deserted beach, the funereal taxis, the diamond of the first star in the immense sky. At the far end of the bay, solitary and enormous at the pier, its lights blazing on every deck, she recognized the ship on which she had sailed, and realized it no longer had anything to do with her life. She turned left at the corner but could not go on because of a crowd being held back by a squad of *carabinieri*. A row of ambulances waited with open doors outside her hotel building.

Standing on tiptoe and peering over the shoulders of the onlookers, Señora Prudencia Linero saw the English tourists again. They were being carried out on stretchers, one by one, and all of them were motionless and dignified and still seemed like one man repeated many times in the more formal clothing they had put on for supper: flannel trousers, diagonally striped ties, and dark jackets with the Trinity College coat of arms embroidered on the breast pocket. As they were brought out, the neighbors watching from their balconies, and the people held back on the street, counted them in chorus as if they were in a stadium. There were seventeen. They were put in the ambulances two by two and driven away to the wail of war sirens.

Dazed by so many stupefying events, Señora Prudencia Linero rode up in the elevator packed with guests from the other hotels who spoke in hermetic languages. They got off at every floor except the third, which was open and lit, but no one was at the counter or in the easy chairs in the foyer where she had seen the pink knees of the seventeen sleeping Englishmen. The owner on the fifth floor commented on the disaster with uncontrolled excitement.

'They're all dead,' she told Señora Prudencia Linero in Spanish. 'They were poisoned by the oyster soup at supper. Just imagine, oysters in August!'

She handed her the key to her room, and paid no further attention to her as she said to the other guests in her own dialect, 'Since there's no dining room here, everyone who goes to sleep wakes up alive!' With another knot of tears in her throat, Señora Prudencia Linero bolted the locks in her room. After that she pushed the little writing table and the easy chair and her trunk against the door to form an impassable barricade against the horror of a country where so many things happened at the same time. Then she put on her widow's nightgown, lay down in the bed on her back, and said seventeen Rosaries for the eternal rest of the souls of the seventeen poisoned Englishmen.

'I Only Came to Use the Phone'

One rainy spring afternoon, while María de la Luz Cervantes was driving alone back to Barcelona, her rented car broke down in the Monegros desert. She was twenty-seven years old, a thoughtful, pretty Mexican who had enjoyed a certain fame as a music hall performer a few years earlier. She was married to a cabaret magician, whom she was to meet later that day after visiting some relatives in Zaragoza. For an hour she made desperate signals to the cars and trucks that sped past her in the storm, until at last the driver of a ramshackle bus took pity on her. He did warn her, however, that he was not going very far.

'It doesn't matter,' said María. 'All I need is a telephone.'

That was true, and she needed it only to let her husband know that she would not be home before seven. Wearing a student's coat and beach shoes in April, she looked like a bedraggled little bird, and she was so distraught after her mishap that she forgot to take the car keys. A woman with a military air was sitting next to the driver, and she gave María a towel and a blanket and made room for her on the seat. María wiped off the worst of the rain and then sat down, wrapped herself in the blanket, and tried to light a cigarette, but her matches were wet. The woman sharing the seat gave her a light and asked for one of the few cigarettes that were still dry. While they smoked, María gave in to a desire to vent her feelings and raised her voice over the noise of the rain and the clatter of the bus. The woman interrupted her by placing a forefinger to her lips.

'They're asleep,' she whispered.

María looked over her shoulder and saw that the bus was full of women of uncertain ages and varying conditions who were sleeping in blankets just like hers. Their serenity was contagious, and María curled up in her seat and succumbed to the sound of the rain. When she awoke, it was dark and the storm had dissolved into an icy drizzle. She had no idea how long she had slept or what place in the world they had come to. Her neighbor looked watchful.

'Where are we?' María asked.

'We've arrived,' answered the woman.

The bus was entering the cobbled courtyard of an enormous, gloomy building that seemed to be an old convent in a forest of colossal trees. The passengers, just visible in the dim light of a lamp in the courtyard, sat motionless until the woman with the military air ordered them out of the bus with the kind of primitive directions used in nursery school. They were all older women, and their movements were so lethargic in the half-light of the courtyard that they looked like images in a dream. María, the last to climb down, thought they were nuns. She was less certain when she saw several women in uniform who received them at the door of the bus, pulled the blankets over their heads to keep them dry, and lined them up single file, directing them not by speaking but with rhythmic, peremptory clapping. María said goodbye and tried to give the blanket to the woman whose seat she had shared, but the woman told her to use it to cover her head while she crossed the courtyard and then return it at the porter's office.

'Is there a telephone?' María asked.

'Of course,' said the woman. 'They'll show you where it is.'

She asked for another cigarette, and María gave her the rest of the damp pack. 'They'll dry on the way,' she said. The woman waved good-bye from the running board, and called 'Good luck' in a voice that was almost a shout. The bus pulled away without giving her time to say anything else.

María started running toward the doorway of the building. A matron tried to stop her with an energetic clap of the hands, but had to resort to an imperious shout: 'Stop, I said!' María looked out from under the blanket and saw a pair of icy eyes and an inescapable forefinger pointing her into the line. She obeyed. Once inside the vestibule she separated from the group and asked the porter where the telephone was. One of the matrons returned her to the line with little pats on the shoulder while she said in a saccharine voice:

'This way, beautiful, the telephone's this way.'

María walked with the other women down a dim corridor until they came to a communal dormitory, where the matrons collected the blankets and began to assign beds. Another matron, who seemed more humane and of higher rank to María, walked down the line comparing a list of names with those written on cardboard tags stitched to the bodices of the new arrivals. When she reached María, she was surprised to see that she was not wearing her identification.

'I only came to use the phone,' María told her.

She explained with great urgency that her car had broken down on the highway. Her husband, who performed magic tricks at parties, was waiting for her in Barcelona because they had three engagements before midnight, and she wanted to let him know she would not be there in time to go with him. It was almost seven o'clock. He had to leave home in ten minutes, and she was afraid he would cancel everything because she was late. The matron appeared to listen to her with attention.

'What's your name?' she asked.

María said her name with a sigh of relief, but the woman did not find it after going over the list several times. With some alarm she questioned another matron, who had nothing to say and shrugged her shoulders.

'But I only came to use the phone,' said María.

'Sure, honey,' the supervisor told her, escorting her to her bed with a sweetness that was too patent to be real, 'if you're good you can call anybody you want. But not now, tomorrow.'

Then something clicked in María's mind, and she understood why the women on the bus moved as if they were on the bottom of an aquarium. They were, in fact, sedated with tranquilizers, and that dark palace with the thick stone walls and frozen stairways was really a hospital for female mental patients. She raced out of the dormitory in dismay, but before she could reach the main door a gigantic matron wearing mechanic's coveralls stopped her with a blow of her huge hand and held her immobile on the floor in an armlock. María, paralyzed with terror, looked at her sideways.

'For the love of God,' she said. 'I swear by my dead mother I only came to use the phone.'

Just one glance at her face was enough for María to know that no amount of pleading would move that maniac in coveralls who was called Herculina because of her uncommon strength. She was in charge of difficult cases, and two inmates had been strangled to death by her polar bear arm skilled in the art of killing by mistake. It was established that the first case had been an accident. The second proved less clear, and Herculina was admonished and warned that the next time she would be subjected to a thorough investigation. The accepted story was that this black sheep of a fine old family had a dubious history of suspicious accidents in various mental hospitals throughout Spain.

They had to inject María with a sedative to make her sleep the first night. When a longing to smoke roused her before dawn, she was tied to the metal bars of the bed by her wrists and ankles. She shouted, but no one came. In the morning, while her husband could find no trace of her in Barcelona, she had to be taken to the infirmary, for they found her senseless in a swamp of her own misery.

When she regained consciousness she did not know how much time had passed. But now the world seemed a haven of love. Beside her bed, a monumental old man with a flatfooted walk and a calming smile gave her back her joy in being alive with two masterful passes of his hand. He was the director of the sanatorium.

Before saying anything to him, without even greeting him, María asked for a cigarette. He lit one and handed it to her, along with the pack, which was almost full. María could not hold back her tears.

'Now is the time to cry to your heart's content,' the doctor said in a soporific voice. 'Tears are the best medicine.'

María unburdened herself without shame, as she had never been able to do with her casual lovers in the empty times that followed lovemaking. As he listened, the doctor smoothed her hair with his fingers, arranged her pillow to ease her breathing, guided her through the labyrinth of her uncertainty with a wisdom and a sweetness she never had dreamed possible. This was, for the first time in her life, the miracle of being understood by a man who listened to her with all his heart and did not expect to go to bed with her as a reward. At the end of a long hour, when she had bared the depths of her soul, she asked permission to speak to her husband on the telephone.

The doctor stood up with all the majesty of his position. 'Not yet, princess,' he said, patting her cheek with more tenderness than she ever had felt before. 'Everything in due course.' He gave her a bishop's blessing from the door, asked her to trust him, and disappeared forever.

That same afternoon María was admitted to the asylum with a serial number and a few superficial comments concerning the enigma of where she had come from and the doubts surrounding her identity. In the margin the director had written an assessment in his own hand: *agitated*.

Just as María had foreseen, her husband left their modest apartment in the Horta district half an hour behind schedule for his three engagements. It was the first time she had been late in the almost two years of their free and very harmonious union, and he assumed it was due to the heavy downpours that had devastated the entire province that weekend. Before he went out he pinned a note to the door with his itinerary for the night.

At the first party, where all the children were dressed in kangaroo costumes, he omitted his best illusion, the invisible fish, because he could not do it without her assistance. His second engagement was in the house of a ninety-three-year-old woman in a wheelchair, who prided herself on having celebrated each of her last thirty birthdays with a different magician. He was so troubled by María's absence that he could not concentrate on the simplest tricks. At his third engagement, the one he did every night at a café on the Ramblas, he gave an uninspired performance for a group of French tourists who could not believe what they saw because they refused to believe in magic. After each show he telephoned his house, and waited in despair for María to answer. After the last call he could no longer control his concern that something had happened to her.

On his way home, in the van adapted for public performances, he saw the splendor of spring in the palm trees along the Paseo de Gracia, and he shuddered at the ominous thought of what the city would be like without María. His last hope vanished when he found his note still pinned to the door. He was so troubled he forgot to feed the cat.

I realize now as I write this that I never learned his real name, because in Barcelona we knew him only by his professional name: Saturno the Magician. He was a man of odd character and irredeemable social awkwardness, but María had more than enough of the tact and charm he lacked. It was she who led him by the hand through this community of great mysteries, where no man would have dreamed of calling after midnight to look for his wife. Saturno had, soon after he arrived, and he preferred to forget the incident. And so that night he settled for calling Zaragoza, where a sleepy grandmother told him with no alarm that María had said goodbye after lunch. He slept for just an hour at dawn. He had a muddled dream in which he saw María wearing a ragged wedding dress spattered with blood, and he woke with the fearful certainty that this time she had left him forever, to face the vast world without her.

She had deserted three different men, including him, in the last five years. She had left him in Mexico City six months after they met, when they were in the throes of pleasure from their demented lovemaking in a maid's room in the Anzures district. One morning, after a night of unspeakable profligacy, María was gone. She left behind everything that was hers, even the ring from her previous marriage, along with a letter in which she said she was incapable of surviving the torment of that wild love. Saturno thought she had returned to her first husband, a high school classmate she had married in secret while still a minor and abandoned for another man after two loveless years. But no: She had gone to her parents' house, and Saturno followed to get her back regardless of the cost. His pleading was unconditional, he made many more promises than he was prepared to keep, but he came up against an invincible determination. 'There are short loves and there are long ones,' she told him. And she concluded with a merciless, 'This was a short one.' Her inflexibility forced him to admit defeat. But in the early hours of the morning of All Saints' Day, when he returned to his orphan's room after almost a year of deliberate forgetting, he found her asleep on the living room sofa with the crown of orange blossoms and long tulle train worn by virgin brides.

María told him the truth. Her new fiancé, a childless widower with a settled life and a mind to marry forever in the Catholic Church, had left her dressed and waiting at the altar. Her parents decided to hold the reception anyway, and she played along with them. She danced, sang with the mariachis, had too much to drink, and in a terrible state of belated remorse left at midnight to find Saturno.

He was not home, but she found the keys in the flower pot in the hall, where they always hid them. Now she was the one whose surrender was unconditional. 'How long this time?' he asked. She answered with a line by Vinicius de Moraes: 'Love is eternal for as long as it lasts.' Two years later, it was still eternal.

María seemed to mature. She renounced her dreams of being an actress and dedicated herself to him, both in work and in bed. At the end of the previous year they had attended a magicians' convention in Perpignan, and on their way home they visited Barcelona for the first time. They liked it so much they had been living here for eight months, and it suited them so well they bought an apartment in the very Catalonian neighborhood of

Horta. It was noisy, and they had no porter, but there was more than enough room for five children. Their happiness was all one could hope for, until the weekend when she rented a car and went to visit her relatives in Zaragoza, promising to be back by seven on Monday night. By dawn on Thursday there was still no word from her.

On Monday of the following week, the insurance company for the rented car called and asked for María. 'I don't know anything,' said Saturno. 'Look for her in Zaragoza.' He hung up. A week later a police officer came to the house to report that the car had been found, stripped bare, on a back road to Cádiz, nine hundred kilometers from the spot where María had abandoned it. The officer wanted to know if she had further details regarding the theft. Saturno was feeding the cat, and he did not look up when he told him straight out that the police shouldn't waste their time because his wife had left him and he didn't know where she had gone or with whom. His conviction was so great that the officer felt uncomfortable and apologized for his questions. They declared the case closed.

The suspicion that María might leave him again had assailed Saturno at Easter in Cadaqués, where Rosa Regás had invited them to go sailing. In the Marítim, the crowded, sordid bar of the *gauche divine* during the twilight of Francoism, twenty of us were squeezed together around one of those wrought-iron tables that had room only for six. After she smoked her second pack of cigarettes of the day, María ran out of matches. A thin, downy arm wearing a Roman bronze bracelet made its way through the noisy crowd at the table and gave her a light. She said thank you without looking at the person she was thanking, but Saturno the Magician saw him – a bony, clean-shaven adolescent as pale as death, with a very black ponytail that hung down to his waist. The windowpanes in the bar just managed to withstand the fury of the spring tramontana wind, but he wore a kind of street pajama made of raw cotton, and a pair of farmer's sandals.

They did not see him again until late autumn, in a seafood bar in La Barceloneta, wearing the same plain cotton outfit and a long braid instead of the ponytail. He greeted them both as if they were old friends, and the way he kissed María, and the way she kissed him back, struck Saturno with the suspicion that they had been seeing each other in secret. Days later he happened to come across a new name and phone number that María had written in their household address book, and the unmerciful lucidity of jealousy revealed to him whose they were. The intruder's background was the final proof: He was twenty-two years old, the only child of a wealthy family, and a decorator of fashionable shop windows, with a casual reputation as a bisexual and a well-founded notoriety as a paid comforter of married women. But Saturno managed to restrain himself until the night María did not come home. Then he began calling him every day, from six in the morning until just before the following dawn, every two or three hours at first, and then whenever he was near a telephone. The fact that no one answered intensified Saturno's martyrdom.

On the fourth day an Andalusian woman who was there just to clean picked up the phone. 'The gentleman's gone away,' she said, with enough vagueness to drive him mad. Saturno did not resist the temptation of asking if Señorita María was in by any chance.

'Nobody named María lives here,' the woman told him. 'The gentleman is a bachelor.'

'I know,' he said. 'She doesn't live there, but sometimes she visits, right?'

The woman became annoyed.

'Who the hell is this, anyway?'

Saturno hung up. The woman's denial seemed one more confirmation of what for him was no longer a suspicion but a burning certainty. He lost control. In the days that followed he called everyone he knew in Barcelona, in alphabetical order. No one could tell him anything, but each call deepened his misery, because his jealous frenzies had become famous among the unrepentant night owls of the *gauche divine*, and they responded with any kind of joke that would make him suffer. Only then did he realize how alone he was in that beautiful, lunatic, impenetrable city, where he would never be happy. At dawn, after he fed the cat, he hardened his heart to keep from dying and resolved to forget María.

After two months María had not yet adjusted to life in the sanatorium. She survived by just picking at the prison rations with flatware chained to the long table of unfinished wood, her eyes fixed on the lithograph of General Francisco Franco that presided over the gloomy medieval dining room. At first she resisted the canonical hours with their mindless routine of matins, lauds, vespers, as well as the other church services that took up most of the time. She refused to play ball in the recreation yard, or to make artificial flowers in the workshop that a group of inmates attended with frenetic diligence. But after the third week she began, little by little, to join in the life of the cloister. After all, said the doctors, every one of them started out the same way, and sooner or later they became integrated into the community.

The lack of cigarettes, resolved in the first few days by a matron who sold them for the price of gold, returned to torment her again when she had spent the little money she had with her. Then she took comfort in the newspaper cigarettes that some inmates made with the butts they picked out of the trash, for her obsessive desire to smoke had become as intense as her fixation on the telephone. Later on, the few pesetas she earned making artificial flowers allowed her an ephemeral consolation.

Hardest of all was her loneliness at night. Many inmates lay awake in the semi-darkness, as she did, not daring to do anything because the night matron at the heavy door secured with a chain and padlock was awake too. One night, however, overcome with grief, María asked in a voice loud enough for the woman in the next bed to hear:

'Where are we?'

The grave, lucid voice of her neighbor answered:

'In the pit of hell.'

'They say this is the country of the Moors,' said another, distant voice that resounded throughout the dormitory. 'And it must be true, because in the summer, when there's a moon, you can hear the dogs barking at the sea.'

The chain running through the locks sounded like

the anchor of a galleon, and the door opened. Their pitiless guardian, the only creature who seemed alive in the instantaneous silence, began walking from one end of the dormitory to the other. María was seized with terror, and only she knew why.

Since her first week in the sanatorium, the night matron had been proposing outright that María sleep with her in the guardroom. She began in a concrete, businesslike tone: an exchange of love for cigarettes, for chocolate, for whatever she wanted. 'You'll have everything,' the matron said, tremulous. 'You'll be the queen.' When María refused, she changed her tactics, leaving little love notes under her pillow, in the pockets of her robe, in the most unexpected places. They were messages of a heart-breaking urgency that could have moved a stone. On the night of the dormitory incident, it had been more than a month that she had seemed resigned to defeat.

When she was certain the other inmates were asleep, the matron approached María's bed and whispered all kinds of tender obscenities in her ear while she kissed her face, her neck tensed with terror, her rigid arms, her exhausted legs. Then, thinking perhaps that María's paralysis stemmed not from fear but from compliance, she dared to go further. That was when María hit her with the back of her hand and sent her crashing into the next bed. The enraged matron stood up in the midst of the uproar created by the agitated inmates.

'You bitch!' she shouted. 'We'll rot together in this hellhole until you go crazy for me.'

Summer arrived without warning on the first Sunday in June, requiring emergency measures because during

Mass the sweltering inmates began taking off their shapeless serge gowns. With some amusement María watched the spectacle of naked patients being chased like blind chickens up and down the aisles by the matrons. In the confusion she tried to protect herself from wild blows, and she somehow found herself alone in an empty office, where the incessant ring of a telephone had a pleading tone. María answered without thinking and heard a distant, smiling voice that took great pleasure in imitating the telephone company's time service:

'The time is forty-five hours, ninety-two minutes, and one hundred seven seconds.'

'Asshole,' said María.

She hung up, amused. She was about to leave when she realized she was allowing a unique opportunity to slip away. She dialed six digits, with so much tension and so much haste she was not sure it was her home number. She waited, her heart racing, she heard the avid, sad sound of the familiar ring, once, twice, three times, and at last she heard the voice of the man she loved, in the house without her.

'Hello?'

She had to wait for the knot of tears that formed in her throat to dissolve.

'Baby, sweetheart,' she sighed.

Her tears overcame her. On the other end of the line there was a brief, horrified silence, and a voice burning with jealousy spit out the word:

'Whore!'

And he slammed down the receiver.

That night, in an attack of rage, María pulled down

the lithograph of the Generalissimo in the refectory, crashed it with all her strength into the stained-glass window that led to the garden, and threw herself to the floor, covered in blood. She still had enough fury left to resist the blows of the matrons who tried, with no success, to restrain her, until she saw Herculina standing in the doorway with her arms folded, staring at her. María gave up. Nevertheless, they dragged her to the ward for violent patients, subdued her with a hose spurting icy water, and injected turpentine into her legs. The swelling that resulted prevented her from walking, and María realized there was nothing in the world she would not do to escape that hell. The following week, when she was back in the dormitory, she tiptoed to the night matron's room and knocked at the door.

María's price, which she demanded in advance, was that the matron send a message to her husband. The matron agreed, on the condition that their dealings be kept an absolute secret. And she pointed an inexorable forefinger at her.

'If they ever find out, you die.'

And so, on the following Saturday, Saturno the Magician drove to the asylum for women in the circus van, which he had prepared to celebrate María's return. The director himself received him in his office, which was as clean and well ordered as a battleship, and made an affectionate report on his wife's condition. No one had known where she came from, or how or when, since the first information regarding her arrival was the official admittance form he had dictated after interviewing her. An investigation begun that same day had proved inconclusive. In any event, what most intrigued the director was how Saturno had learned his wife's whereabouts. Saturno protected the matron.

'The insurance company told me,' he said.

The director nodded, satisfied. 'I don't know how insurance companies manage to find out everything,' he said. He looked over the file lying on his ascetic's desk, and concluded:

'The only certainty is the seriousness of her condition.'

He was prepared to authorize a visit with all the necessary precautions if Saturno the Magician would promise, for the good of his wife, to adhere without question to the rules of behavior that he would indicate. Above all with reference to how he treated her, in order to avoid a recurrence of the fits of rage that were becoming more and more frequent and dangerous.

'How strange,' said Saturno. 'She always was quick-tempered, but had a lot of self-control.'

The doctor made a learned man's gesture. 'There are behaviors that remain latent for many years, and then one day they erupt,' he said. 'All in all, it is fortunate she happened to come here, because we specialize in cases requiring a firm hand.' Then he warned him about María's strange obsession with the telephone.

'Humor her,' he said.

'Don't worry, Doctor,' Saturno said with a cheerful air. 'That's my specialty.'

The visiting room, a combination of prison cell and confessional, was the former locutory of the convent. Saturno's entrance was not the explosion of joy they both might have expected. María stood in the middle of the room, next to a small table with two chairs and a vase empty of flowers. It was obvious she was ready to leave, with her lamentable strawberry-colored coat and a pair of disreputable shoes given to her out of charity. Herculina stood in a corner, almost invisible, her arms folded. María did not move when she saw her husband come in, and her face, still marked by the shattered window glass, showed no emotion. They exchanged routine kisses.

'How do you feel?' he asked her.

'Happy you're here at last, baby,' she said. 'This has been death.'

They did not have time to sit down. Drowning in tears, María told him about the miseries of the cloister, the brutality of the matrons, the food not fit for dogs, the endless nights when terror kept her from closing her eyes.

'I don't even know how many days I've been here, or how many months or years, all I know is that each one has been worse than the last,' and she sighed with all her soul. 'I don't think I'll ever be the same.'

'That's all over now,' he said, caressing the recent scars on her face with his fingertips. 'I'll come every Saturday. More often than that, if the director lets me. You'll see, everything will turn out just fine.'

She fixed her terrified eyes on his. Saturno tried to use his performer's charm. He told her, in the puerile tone of all great lies, a sweetened version of the doctor's prognosis. 'It means,' he concluded, 'that you still need a few more days to make a complete recovery.' María understood the truth.

'For God's sake, baby,' she said, stunned. 'Don't tell me you think I'm crazy too!'

'The things you think of!' he said, trying to laugh. 'But it really will be much better for everybody if you stay here a while. Under better conditions, of course.'

'But I've already told you I only came to use the phone!' said María.

He did not know how to react to her dreadful obsession. He looked at Herculina. She took advantage of the opportunity to point at her wristwatch as a sign that it was time to end the visit. María intercepted the signal, glanced behind her, and saw Herculina tensing for an imminent attack. Then she clung to her husband's neck, screaming like a real madwoman. He freed himself with as much love as he could muster, and left her to the mercies of Herculina, who jumped her from behind. Without giving María time to react, she applied an armlock with her left hand, put her other iron arm around her throat, and shouted at Saturno the Magician:

'Leave!'

Saturno fled in terror.

But on the following Saturday, when he had recovered from the shock of the visit, he returned to the sanatorium with the cat, which he had dressed in an outfit identical to his: the red-and-yellow tights of the great Leotardo, a top hat, and a swirling cape that seemed made for flying. He drove the circus van into the courtyard of the cloister, and there he put on a prodigious show lasting almost three hours, which the inmates enjoyed from the balconies with discordant shouts and inopportune applause. They were all there except María, who not only refused to receive her husband but would not even watch him from the balconies. Saturno felt wounded to the quick.

'It is a typical reaction,' the director consoled him. 'It will pass.'

But it never passed. After attempting many times to see María again, Saturno did all he could to have her accept a letter from him, but to no avail. She returned it four times, unopened and with no comments. Saturno gave up but continued leaving a supply of cigarettes at the porter's office without ever finding out if they reached María, until at last reality defeated him.

No one heard any more about him except that he married again and returned to his own country. Before leaving Barcelona he gave the half-starved cat to a casual girlfriend, who also promised to take cigarettes to María. But she disappeared too. Rosa Regás remembered seeing her in the Corte Inglés department store about twelve years ago, with the shaved head and orange robes of some Oriental sect, and very pregnant. She told Rosa she had taken cigarettes to María as often as she could, and settled some unforeseen emergencies for her, until one day she found only the ruins of the hospital, which had been demolished like a bad memory of those wretched times. María seemed very lucid on her last visit, a little overweight, and content with the peace of the cloister. That was the day she also brought María the cat, because she had spent all the money that Saturno had given her for its food.

The Woman Who Came at Six O'Clock

The swinging door opened. At that hour there was nobody in José's restaurant. It had just struck six and the man knew that the regular customers wouldn't begin to arrive until six-thirty. His clientele was so conservative and regular that the clock hadn't finished striking six when a woman entered, as on every day at that hour, and sat down on the stool without saying anything. She had an unlighted cigarette tight between her lips.

'Hello, queen,' José said when he saw her sit down. Then he went to the other end of the counter, wiping the streaked surface with a dry rag. Whenever anyone came into the restaurant José did the same thing. Even with the woman, with whom he'd almost come to acquire a degree of intimacy, the fat and ruddy restaurant owner put on his daily comedy of a hard-working man. He spoke from the other end of the counter.

'What do you want today?' he said.

'First of all I want to teach you how to be a gentleman,' the woman said. She was sitting at the end of the stools, her elbows on the counter, the extinguished cigarette between her lips. When she spoke, she tightened her mouth so that José would notice the unlighted cigarette.

'I didn't notice,' José said.

'You still haven't learned to notice anything,' said the woman.

The man left the cloth on the counter, walked to the

dark cupboards which smelled of tar and dusty wood, and came back immediately with the matches. The woman leaned over to get the light that was burning in the man's rustic, hairy hands. José saw the woman's lush hair, all greased with cheap, thick Vaseline. He saw her uncovered shoulder above the flowered brassiere. He saw the beginning of her twilight breast when the woman raised her head, the lighted butt between her lips now.

'You're beautiful tonight, queen,' José said.

'Stop your nonsense,' the woman said. 'Don't think that's going to help me pay you.'

'That's not what I meant, queen,' José said. 'I'll bet your lunch didn't agree with you today.'

The woman sucked in the first drag of thick smoke, crossed her arms, her elbows still on the counter, and remained looking at the street through the wide restaurant window. She had a melancholy expression. A bored and vulgar melancholy.

'I'll fix you a good steak,' José said.

'I still haven't got any money,' the woman said.

'You haven't had any money for three months and I always fix you something good,' José said.

'Today's different,' said the woman somberly, still looking out at the street.

'Every day's the same,' José said. 'Every day the clock says six, then you come in and say you're hungry as a dog and then I fix you something good. The only difference is this: today you didn't say you were as hungry as a dog but that today is different.'

'And it's true,' the woman said. She turned to look at the man, who was at the other end of the counter checking the refrigerator. She examined him for two or three seconds. Then she looked at the clock over the cupboard. It was three minutes after six. 'It's true, José. Today is different,' she said. She let the smoke out and kept on talking with crisp, impassioned words. 'I didn't come at six today, that's why it's different, José.'

The man looked at the clock.

'I'll cut off my arm if that clock is one minute slow,' he said.

'That's not it, José. I didn't come at six o'clock today,' the woman said.

'It just struck six, queen,' José said. 'When you came in it was just finishing.'

'I've got a quarter of an hour that says I've been here,' the woman said.

José went over to where she was. He put his great puffy face up to the woman while he tugged on one of his eyelids with his index finger.

'Blow on me here,' he said.

The woman threw her head back. She was serious, annoyed, softened, beautified by a cloud of sadness and fatigue.

'Stop your foolishness, José. You know I haven't had a drink for six months.'

'Tell it to somebody else,' he said, 'not to me. I'll bet you've had a pint or two at least.'

'I had a couple of drinks with a friend,' she said.

'Oh, now I understand,' José said.

'There's nothing to understand,' the woman said. 'I've been here for a quarter of an hour.'

The man shrugged his shoulders.

'Well, if that's the way you want it, you've got a quarter of an hour that says you've been here,' he said.

'After all, what difference does it make, ten minutes this way, ten minutes that way?'

'It makes a difference, José,' the woman said. And she stretched her arms over the glass counter with an air of careless abandon. She said: 'And it isn't that I wanted it that way; it's just that I've been here for a quarter of an hour.' She looked at the clock again and corrected herself: 'What am I saying – it's been twenty minutes.'

'O.K., queen,' the man said. 'I'd give you a whole day and the night that goes with it just to see you happy.'

During all this time José had been moving about behind the counter, changing things, taking something from one place and putting it in another. He was playing his role.

'I want to see you happy,' he repeated. He stopped suddenly, turning to where the woman was. 'Do you know that I love you very much?'

The woman looked at him coldly.

'Ye-e-es . . . ? What a discovery, José. Do you think I'd go with you even for a million pesos?'

'I didn't mean that, queen,' José said. 'I repeat, I bet your lunch didn't agree with you.'

'That's not why I said it,' the woman said. And her voice became less indolent. 'No woman could stand a weight like yours, even for a million pesos.'

José blushed. He turned his back to the woman and began to dust the bottles on the shelves. He spoke without turning his head.

'You're unbearable today, queen. I think the best thing is for you to eat your steak and go home to bed.'

'I'm not hungry,' the woman said. She stayed looking out at the street again, watching the passers-by of the dusking city. For an instant there was a murky silence in the restaurant. A peacefulness broken only by José's fiddling about in the cupboard. Suddenly the woman stopped looking out into the street and spoke with a tender, soft, different voice.

'Do you really love me, Pepillo?'

'I do,' José said dryly, not looking at her.

'In spite of what I've said to you?' the woman asked.

'What did you say to me?' José asked, still without any inflection in his voice, still without looking at her.

'That business about a million pesos,' the woman said.

'I'd already forgotten,' José said.

'So do you love me?' the woman asked.

'Yes,' said José.

There was a pause. José kept moving about, his face turned towards the cabinets, still not looking at the woman. She blew out another mouthful of smoke, rested her bust on the counter, and then, cautiously roguishly, biting her tongue before saying it, as if speaking on tiptoe:

'Even if you didn't go to bed with me?' she asked.

And only then did José turn to look at her.

'I love you so much that I wouldn't go to bed with you,' he said. Then he walked over to where she was. He stood looking into her face, his powerful arms leaning on the counter in front of her, looking into her eyes. He said: 'I love you so much that every night I'd kill the man who goes with you.'

At the first instant the woman seemed perplexed. Then she looked at the man attentively, with a wavering expression of compassion and mockery. Then she had a moment of brief disconcerted silence. And then she laughed noisily.

'You're jealous, José. That's wild, you're jealous!'

José blushed again with frank, almost shameful timidity, as might have happened to a child who'd revealed all his secrets all of a sudden. He said:

'This afternoon you don't seem to understand anything, queen.' And he wiped himself with the rag. He said:

'This bad life is brutalizing you.'

But now the woman had changed her expression.

'So, then,' she said. And she looked into his eyes again, with a strange glow in her look, confused and challenging at the same time.

'So you're not jealous.'

'In a way I am,' José said. 'But it's not the way you think.'

He loosened his collar and continued wiping himself, drying his throat with the cloth.

'So?' the woman asked.

'The fact is I love you so much that I don't like your doing it,' José said.

'What?' the woman asked.

'This business of going with a different man every day,' José said.

'Would you really kill him to stop him from going with me?' the woman asked.

'Not to stop him from going with you, no,' José said. 'I'd kill him because he *went* with you.'

'It's the same thing,' the woman said.

The conversation had reached an exciting density. The woman was speaking in a soft, low, fascinated voice.

Her face was almost stuck up against the man's healthy, peaceful face, as he stood motionless, as if bewitched by the vapor of the words.

'That's true,' José said.

'So,' the woman said, and reached out her hand to stroke the man's rough arm. With the other she tossed away her butt. 'So you're capable of killing a man?'

'For what I told you, yes,' José said. And his voice took on an almost dramatic stress.

The woman broke into convulsive laughter, with an obvious mocking intent.

'How awful, José. How awful,' she said, still laughing. 'José killing a man. Who would have known that behind the fat and sanctimonious man who never makes me pay, who cooks me a steak every day and has fun talking to me until I find a man, there lurks a murderer. How awful, José! You scare me!'

José was confused. Maybe he felt a little indignation. Maybe, when the woman started laughing, he felt defrauded.

'You're drunk, silly,' he said. 'Go get some sleep. You don't even feel like eating anything.'

But the woman had stopped laughing now and was serious again, pensive, leaning on the counter. She watched the man go away. She saw him open the refrigerator and close it again without taking anything out. Then she saw him move to the other end of the counter. She watched him polish the shining glass, the same as in the beginning. Then the woman spoke again with the tender and soft tone of when she said: 'Do you really love me, Pepillo?'

'José,' she said.

The man didn't look at her.

'José!'

'Go home and sleep,' José said. 'And take a bath before you go to bed so you can sleep it off.'

'Seriously, José,' the woman said. 'I'm not drunk.'

'Then you've turned stupid,' José said.

'Come here, I've got to talk to you,' the woman said.

The man came over stumbling, halfway between pleasure and mistrust.

'Come closer!'

He stood in front of the woman again. She leaned forward, grabbed him by the hair, but with a gesture of obvious tenderness.

'Tell me again what you said at the start,' she said.

'What do you mean?' José asked. He was trying to look at her with his head turned away, held by the hair.

'That you'd kill a man who went to bed with me,' the woman said.

'I'd kill a man who went to bed with you, queen. That's right,' José said.

The woman let him go.

'In that case you'd defend me if I killed him, right?' she asked affirmatively, pushing José's enormous pig head with a movement of brutal coquettishness. The man didn't answer anything. He smiled.

'Answer me, José,' the woman said. 'Would you defend me if I killed him?'

'That depends,' José said. 'You know it's not as easy as you say.'

'The police wouldn't believe anyone more than you,' the woman said.

José smiled, honored, satisfied. The woman leaned over toward him again, over the counter.

'It's true, José. I'm willing to bet that you've never told a lie in your life,' she said.

'You won't get anywhere this way,' José said.

'Just the same,' the woman said. 'The police know you and they'll believe anything without asking you twice.'

José began pounding on the counter opposite her, not knowing what to say. The woman looked out at the street again. Then she looked at the clock and modified the tone of her voice, as if she were interested in finishing the conversation before the first customers arrived.

'Would you tell a lie for me, José?' she asked. 'Seriously.'

And then José looked at her again, sharply, deeply, as if a tremendous idea had come pounding up in his head. An idea that had entered through one ear, spun about for a moment, vague, confused, and gone out through the other, leaving behind only a warm vestige of terror.

'What have you got yourself into, queen?' José asked. He leaned forward, his arms folded over the counter again. The woman caught the strong and ammonia-smelling vapor of his breathing, which had become difficult because of the pressure that the counter was exercising on the man's stomach.

'This is really serious, queen. What have you got yourself into?' he asked.

The woman made her head spin in the opposite direction.

'Nothing,' she said. 'I was just talking to amuse myself.'

Then she looked at him again.

'Do you know you may not have to kill anybody?'

'I never thought about killing anybody,' José said, distressed.

'No, man,' the woman said. 'I mean nobody goes to bed with me.'

'Oh!' José said. 'Now you're talking straight out. I always thought you had no need to prowl around. I'll make a bet that if you drop all this I'll give you the biggest steak I've got every day, free.'

'Thank you, José,' the woman said. 'But that's not why. It's because I *can't* go to bed with anyone any more.'

'You're getting things all confused again,' José said. He was becoming impatient.

'I'm not getting anything confused,' the woman said. She stretched out on the seat and José saw her flat, sad breasts underneath her brassiere.

'Tomorrow I'm going away and I promise you I won't come back and bother you ever again. I promise you I'll never go to bed with anyone.'

'Where'd you pick up that fever?' José asked.

'I decided just a minute ago,' the woman said. 'Just a minute ago I realized it's a dirty business.'

José grabbed the cloth again and started to clean the glass in front of her. He spoke without looking at her.

He said:

'Of course, the way you do it it's a dirty business. You should have known that a long time ago.'

'I was getting to know it a long time ago,' the woman said, 'but I was only convinced of it just a little while ago. Men disgust me.'

José smiled. He raised his head to look at her, still

smiling, but he saw her concentrated, perplexed, talking with her shoulders raised, twirling on the stool with a taciturn expression, her face gilded by premature autumnal grain.

'Don't you think they ought to lay off a woman who kills a man because after she's been with him she feels disgust with him and everyone who's been with her?'

'There's no reason to go that far,' José said, moved, a thread of pity in his voice.

'What if the woman tells the man he disgusts her while she watches him get dressed because she remembers that she's been rolling around with him all afternoon and feels that neither soap nor sponge can get his smell off her?'

'That all goes away, queen,' José said, a little indifferent now, polishing the counter. 'There's no reason to kill him. Just let him go.'

But the woman kept on talking, and her voice was a uniform, flowing, passionate current.

'But what if the woman tells him he disgusts her and the man stops getting dressed and runs over to her again, kisses her again, does . . . ?'

'No decent man would ever do that,' José says.

'What if he does?' the woman asks, with exasperating anxiety. 'What if the man isn't decent and does it and then the woman feels that he disgusts her so much that she could die, and she knows that the only way to end it all is to stick a knife in under him?'

'That's terrible,' José said. 'Luckily there's no man who would do what you say.'

'Well,' the woman said, completely exasperated now. 'What if he did? Suppose he did.'

'In any case it's not that bad,' José said. He kept on cleaning the counter without changing position, less intent on the conversation now.

The woman pounded the counter with her knuckles. She became affirmative, emphatic.

'You're a savage, José,' she said. 'You don't understand anything.' She grabbed him firmly by the sleeve. 'Come on, tell me that the woman should kill him.'

'O.K.,' José said with a conciliatory bias. 'It's all probably just the way you say it is.'

'Isn't that self-defense?' the woman asked, grabbing him by the sleeve.

Then José gave her a lukewarm and pleasant look.

'Almost, almost,' he said. And he winked at her, with an expression that was at the same time a cordial comprehension and a fearful compromise of complicity. But the woman was serious. She let go of him.

'Would you tell a lie to defend a woman who does that?' she asked.

'That depends,' said José.

'Depends on what?' the woman asked.

'Depends on the woman,' said José.

'Suppose it's a woman you love a lot,' the woman said. 'Not to be with her, but like you say, you love her a lot.'

'O.K., anything you say, queen,' José said, relaxed, bored.

He'd gone off again. He'd looked at the clock. He'd seen that it was going on half-past six. He'd thought that in a few minutes the restaurant would be filling up with people and maybe that was why he began to polish the glass with greater effort, looking at the street through the window. The woman stayed on her stool, silent, concentrating, watching the man's movements with an air of declining sadness. Watching him as a lamp about to go out might have looked at a man. Suddenly, without reacting, she spoke again with the unctuous voice of servitude.

'José!'

The man looked at her with a thick, sad tenderness, like a maternal ox. He didn't look at her to hear her, just to look at her, to know that she was there, waiting for a look that had no reason to be one of protection or solidarity. Just the look of a plaything.

'I told you I was leaving tomorrow and you didn't say anything,' the woman said.

'Yes,' José said. 'You didn't tell me where.'

'Out there,' the woman said. 'Where there aren't any men who want to sleep with somebody.'

José smiled again.

'Are you really going away?' he asked, as if becoming aware of life, quickly changing the expression on his face.

'That depends on you,' the woman said. 'If you know enough to say what time I got here, I'll go away tomorrow and I'll never get mixed up in this again. Would you like that?'

José gave an affirmative nod, smiling and concrete. The woman leaned over to where he was.

'If I come back here someday I'll get jealous when I find another woman talking to you, at this time and on this same stool.'

'If you come back here you'll have to bring me something,' José said.

'I promise you that I'll look everywhere for the tame bear, bring him to you,' the woman said.

José smiled and waved the cloth through the air that separated him from the woman, as if he were cleaning an invisible pane of glass. The woman smiled too, with an expression of cordiality and coquetry now. Then the man went away, polishing the glass to the other end of the counter.

'What, then?' José said without looking at her.

'Will you really tell anyone who asks you that I got here at a quarter to six?' the woman said.

'What for?' José said, still without looking at her now, as if he had barely heard her.

'That doesn't matter,' the woman said. 'The thing is that you do it.'

José then saw the first customer come in through the swinging door and walk over to a corner table. He looked at the clock. It was six-thirty on the dot.

'O.K., queen,' he said distractedly. 'Anything you say. I always do whatever you want.'

'Well,' the woman said. 'Start cooking my steak, then.'

The man went to the refrigerator, took out a plate with a piece of meat on it, and left it on the table. Then he lighted the stove.

'I'm going to cook you a good farewell steak, queen,' he said.

'Thank you, Pepillo,' the woman said.

She remained thoughtful as if suddenly she had become sunken in a strange subworld peopled with muddy, unknown forms. Across the counter she couldn't hear the noise that the raw meat made when it fell into the burning grease. Afterward she didn't hear the dry and bubbling crackle as José turned the flank over in the frying pan and the succulent smell of the marinated meat by measured moments saturated the air of the restaurant. She remained like that, concentrated, reconcentrated, until she raised her head again, blinking as if she were coming back out of a momentary death. Then she saw the man beside the stove, lighted up by the happy, rising fire.

'Pepillo.'

'What!'

'What are you thinking about?' the woman asked.

'I was wondering whether you could find the little windup bear someplace,' José said.

'Of course I can,' the woman said. 'But what I want is for you to give me everything I asked for as a going-away present.'

José looked at her from the stove.

'How often have I got to tell you?' he said. 'Do you want something besides the best steak I've got?'

'Yes,' the woman said.

'What is it?' José asked.

'I want another quarter of an hour.'

José drew back and looked at the clock. Then he looked at the customer, who was still silent, waiting in the corner, and finally at the meat roasting in the pan. Only then did he speak.

'I really don't understand, queen,' he said.

'Don't be foolish, José,' the woman said. 'Just remember that I've been here since five-thirty.'

Light is Like Water

At Christmas the boys asked again for a rowboat.

'Okay,' said their papa, 'we'll buy it when we get back to Cartagena.'

Totó, who was nine years old, and Joel, who was seven, were more determined than their parents believed.

'No,' they said in chorus. 'We need it here and now.'

'To begin with,' said their mother, 'the only navigable water here is what comes out of the shower.'

She and her husband were both right. Their house in Cartagena de Indias had a yard with a dock on the bay, and a shed that could hold two large yachts. Here in Madrid, on the other hand, they were crowded into a fifth-floor apartment at 47 Paseo de la Castellana. But in the end neither of them could refuse, because they had promised the children a rowboat complete with sextant and compass if they won their class prizes in elementary school, and they had. And so their papa bought everything and said nothing to his wife, who was more reluctant than he to pay gambling debts. It was a beautiful aluminum boat with a gold stripe at the waterline.

'The boat's in the garage,' their papa announced at lunch. 'The problem is, there's no way to bring it up in the elevator or by the stairs, and there's no more space available in the garage.'

On the following Saturday afternoon, however, the

boys invited their classmates to help bring the boat up the stairs, and they managed to carry it as far as the maid's room.

'Congratulations,' said their papa. 'Now what?'

'Now nothing,' said the boys. 'All we wanted was to have the boat in the room, and now it's there.'

On Wednesday night, as they did every Wednesday, the parents went to the movies. The boys, lords and masters of the house, closed the doors and windows and broke the glowing bulb in one of the living room lamps. A jet of golden light as cool as water began to pour out of the broken bulb, and they let it run to a depth of almost three feet. Then they turned off the electricity, took out the rowboat, and navigated at will among the islands in the house.

This fabulous adventure was the result of a frivolous remark I made while taking part in a seminar on the poetry of household objects. Totó asked me why the light went on with just the touch of a switch, and I did not have the courage to think about it twice.

'Light is like water,' I answered. 'You turn the tap and out it comes.'

And so they continued sailing every Wednesday night, learning how to use the sextant and the compass, until their parents came home from the movies and found them sleeping like angels on dry land. Months later, longing to go farther, they asked for complete skin-diving outfits: masks, fins, tanks, and compressed-air rifles.

'It's bad enough you've put a rowboat you can't use in the maid's room,' said their father. 'To make it even worse, now you want diving equipment too.'

'What if we win the Gold Gardenia Prize for the first semester?' said Joel.

'No,' said their mother in alarm. 'That's enough.'

Their father reproached her for being intransigent.

'These kids don't win so much as a nail when it comes to doing what they're supposed to,' she said, 'but to get what they want they're capable of taking it all, even the teacher's chair.'

In the end the parents did not say yes or no. But in July, Totó and Joel each won a Gold Gardenia and the public recognition of the headmaster. That same afternoon, without having to ask again, they found the diving outfits in their original packing in their bedroom. And so the following Wednesday, while their parents were at the movies seeing *Last Tango in Paris*, they filled the apartment to a depth of two fathoms, dove like tame sharks under the furniture, including the beds, and salvaged from the bottom of the light things that had been lost in darkness for years.

At the end-of-the-year awards ceremony, the brothers were acclaimed as examples for the entire school and received certificates of excellence. This time they did not have to ask for anything, because their parents asked them what they wanted. They were so reasonable that all they wanted was a party at home as a treat for their classmates.

Their papa, when he was alone with his wife, was radiant.

'It's a proof of their maturity,' he said.

'From your lips to God's ear,' said their mother.

The following Wednesday, while their parents were watching *The Battle of Algiers*, people walking along the

Paseo de la Castellana saw a cascade of light falling from an old building hidden among the trees. It spilled over the balconies, poured in torrents down the façade, and rushed along the great avenue in a golden flood that lit the city all the way to the Guadarrama.

In response to the emergency, firemen forced the door on the fifth floor and found the apartment brimming with light all the way to the ceiling. The sofa and easy chairs covered in leopard skin were floating at different levels in the living room, among the bottles from the bar and the grand piano with its Manila shawl that fluttered half submerged like a golden manta ray. Household objects, in the fullness of their poetry, flew with their own wings through the kitchen sky. The marching-band instruments that the children used for dancing drifted among the bright-colored fish freed from their mother's aquarium, which were the only creatures alive and happy in the vast illuminated marsh. Everyone's toothbrush floated in the bathroom, along with Papa's condoms and Mama's jars of creams and her spare bridge, and the television set from the master bedroom floated on its side, still tuned to the final episode of the midnight movie for adults only.

At the end of the hall, moving with the current and clutching the oars, with his mask on and only enough air to reach port, Totó sat in the stern of the boat, searching for the lighthouse, and Joel, floating in the prow, still looked for the north star with the sextant, and floating through the entire house were their thirty-seven classmates, eternalized in the moment of peeing into the pot of geraniums, singing the school song with the words changed to make fun of the headmaster, sneaking a glass of brandy from Papa's bottle. For they had turned on so many lights at the same time that the apartment had flooded, and two entire classes at the elementary school of Saint Julian the Hospitaler drowned on the fifth floor of 47 Paseo de la Castellana. In Madrid, Spain, a remote city of burning summers and icy winds, with no ocean or river, whose landbound indigenous population had never mastered the science of navigating on light.

POCKET PENGUINS

1. Lady Chatterley's Trial
2. **Eric Schlosser** Cogs in the Great Machine
3. **Nick Hornby** Otherwise Pandemonium
4. **Albert Camus** Summer in Algiers
5. **P. D. James** Innocent House
6. **Richard Dawkins** The View from Mount Improbable
7. **India Knight** On Shopping
8. **Marian Keyes** Nothing Bad Ever Happens in Tiffany's
9. **Jorge Luis Borges** The Mirror of Ink
10. **Roald Dahl** A Taste of the Unexpected
11. **Jonathan Safran Foer** The Unabridged Pocketbook of Lightning
12. **Homer** The Cave of the Cyclops
13. **Paul Theroux** Two Stars
14. **Elizabeth David** Of Pageants and Picnics
15. **Anaïs Nin** Artists and Models
16. **Antony Beevor** Christmas at Stalingrad
17. **Gustave Flaubert** The Desert and the Dancing Girls
18. **Anne Frank** The Secret Annexe
19. **James Kelman** Where I Was
20. **Hari Kunzru** Noise
21. **Simon Schama** The Bastille Falls
22. **William Trevor** The Dressmaker's Child
23. **George Orwell** In Defence of English Cooking
24. **Michael Moore** Idiot Nation
25. **Helen Dunmore** Rose, 1944
26. **J. K. Galbraith** The Economics of Innocent Fraud
27. **Gervase Phinn** The School Inspector Calls
28. **W. G. Sebald** Young Austerlitz
29. **Redmond O'Hanlon** Borneo and the Poet
30. **Ali Smith** Ali Smith's Supersonic 70s
31. **Sigmund Freud** Forgetting Things
32. **Simon Armitage** King Arthur in the East Riding
33. **Hunter S. Thompson** Happy Birthday, Jack Nicholson
34. **Vladimir Nabokov** Cloud, Castle, Lake
35. **Niall Ferguson** 1914: Why the World Went to War

POCKET PENGUINS

36. **Muriel Spark** The Snobs
37. **Steven Pinker** Hotheads
38. **Tony Harrison** Under the Clock
39. **John Updike** Three Trips
40. **Will Self** Design Faults in the Volvo 760 Turbo
41. **H. G. Wells** The Country of the Blind
42. **Noam Chomsky** Doctrines and Visions
43. **Jamie Oliver** Something for the Weekend
44. **Virginia Woolf** Street Haunting
45. **Zadie Smith** Martha and Hanwell
46. **John Mortimer** The Scales of Justice
47. **F. Scott Fitzgerald** The Diamond as Big as the Ritz
48. **Roger McGough** The State of Poetry
49. **Ian Kershaw** Death in the Bunker
50. **Gabriel García Márquez** Seventeen Poisoned Englishmen
51. **Steven Runciman** The Assault on Jerusalem
52. **Sue Townsend** The Queen in Hell Close
53. **Primo Levi** Iron Potassium Nickel
54. **Alistair Cooke** Letters from Four Seasons
55. **William Boyd** Protobiography
56. **Robert Graves** Caligula
57. **Melissa Bank** The Worst Thing a Suburban Girl Could Imagine
58. **Truman Capote** My Side of the Matter
59. **David Lodge** Scenes of Academic Life
60. **Anton Chekhov** The Kiss
61. **Claire Tomalin** Young Bysshe
62. **David Cannadine** The Aristocratic Adventurer
63. **P. G. Wodehouse** Jeeves and the Impending Doom
64. **Franz Kafka** The Great Wall of China
65. **Dave Eggers** Short Short Stories
66. **Evelyn Waugh** The Coronation of Haile Selassie
67. **Pat Barker** War Talk
68. **Jonathan Coe** 9th & 13th
69. **John Steinbeck** Murder
70. **Alain de Botton** On Seeing and Noticing